Piglet and Mama

by Margaret Wild

illustrated by
Stephen Michael King

ABRAMS BOOKS FOR YOUNG READERS, NEW YORK

For Karen & Olivia   —M.W.

For Enya   —S.M.K.

Stephen Michael King used watercolor and black ink for the illustrations in this book.

Library of Congress Cataloging-in-Publication Data

Wild, Margaret, 1948-
Piglet and Mama / by Margaret Wild.
p. cm.
Summary: When Piglet cannot find her mother, all of the barnyard animals try to make her feel better, but Piglet wants nothing but Mama.
Original ISBN 0-8109-5869-4
[1. Mother and child—Fiction. 2. Pigs—Fiction. 3. Domestic animals—Fiction. 4. Farm life—Fiction.]   I. Title.

PZ7.W64574Pi 2005
[E]—dc22
2004019497

ISBN 13: 978-0-8109-5869-2
ISBN 10: 0-8109-5869-4
Text copyright © 2004 Margaret Wild
Illustrations copyright © 2004 Stephen Michael King
First published in Australia by Working Title Press.

Originally published in 2005 by Harry N. Abrams, Inc., New York.
This edition published in 2007 by Abrams Books for Young Readers, an imprint of Harry N. Abrams, Inc.

Printed and bound in Singapore
10 9 8 7 6 5 4 3

HNA
harry n. abrams, inc.
a subsidiary of La Martinière Groupe

115 West 18th Street
New York, NY 10011
www.hnabooks.com

One morning in the farmyard,
Piglet lost her mama.

"Oiiiiiink!" cried Piglet.
So with a snuffle and a snort,
off she went to look for her mama.

"Mama!" said Piglet.

"Your mama's not here," said Duck.

"Let's have a cuddle."

But Piglet wanted her mama.

"Mama!" said Piglet.

"Your mama's not here," said Sheep.

"Let's make a daisy chain."

But Piglet wanted her mama.

"Mama!" said Piglet.

"Your mama's not here," said Donkey.

"Let's play chase."

But Piglet wanted her mama.

"Mama!" said Piglet.

"Your mama's not here," said Dog.

"Let's roll in the mud."

But Piglet wanted her mama.

"Mama!" said Piglet.

"Your mama's not here," said Horse.

"Let's dance in the daffodils."

But Piglet wanted her mama.

"Mama!" said Piglet.

"Your mama's not here," said Cat.

"Let's snooze in the sun."

But Piglet wanted her mama.

"Oiiiiiink!" cried Piglet.

"Oiiiiiink!
There you are!" said Mama. "I've
been looking everywhere for you."

So with a snuffle and a snort,
Piglet and Mama had a
big pig cuddle.

Then they made
a daisy chain,

played chase,

rolled in the mud,

danced
in
the
daffodils . . .

and snoozed side by side in the sun.